Young Learner's

My Favourite Stories

Wishes are Unending
The Backyard Fence

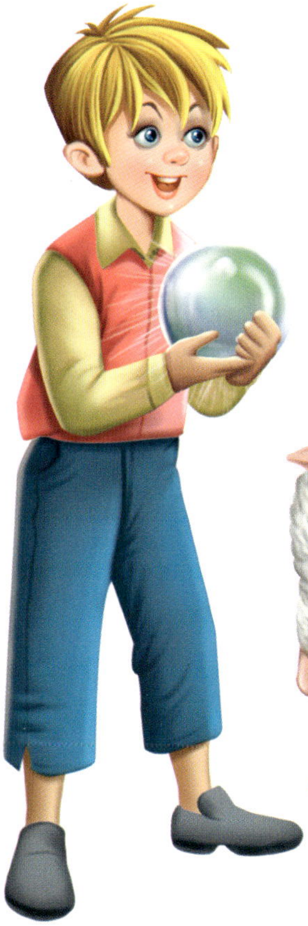

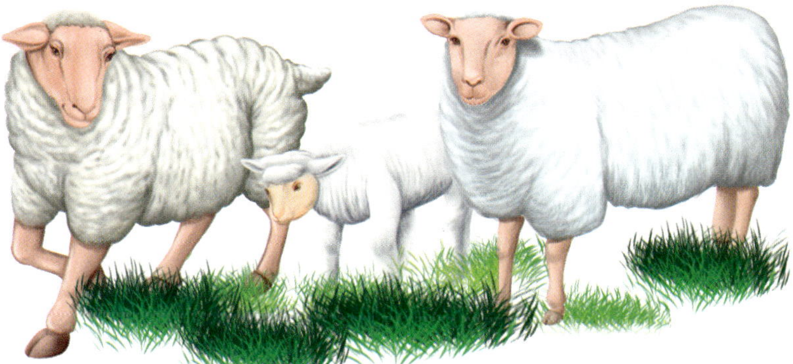

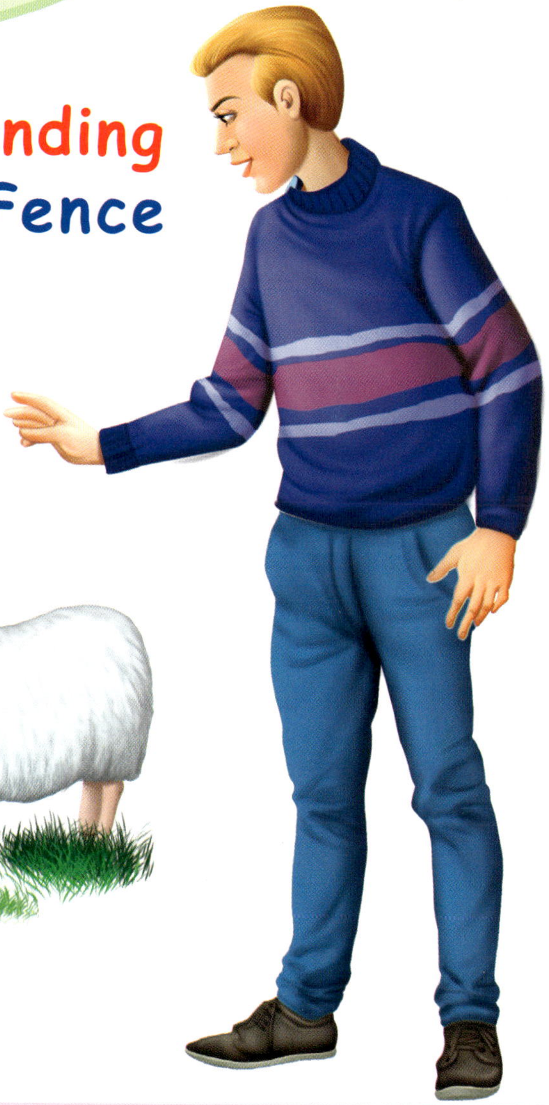

Wishes are Unending

A boy called Ivan lived in a small village in Spain. Nestled in a beautiful valley, the village was full of happiness and love. The children spent their evenings playing with each other. The adults too, were fond of each other and often ate their meals together.

Every morning, Ivan took his herd to the lush green pastures for grazing. While the sheep grazed he played his flute. By afternoon, he would return home. After lunch, he would play with his friends.

One day, Ivan saw a bright light in the bushes. He went nearer and was surprised to see a shining crystal ball. He picked it up and looked at it in wonder. Suddenly, the ball spoke, “Make a wish and I shall fulfill it!” Ivan thought hard but could think of nothing to wish for. He said to the ball, “I shall tell you later what I want.” He put the ball in his bag and carried it home.

Days passed but Ivan could think of nothing to wish for. One day, Ivan's friend Gonzalo also went along with him to the pasture. As the sheep grazed, Ivan took out the crystal ball from his bag and showed it to Gonzalo. Now, Gonzalo was a greedy boy. He insisted upon asking for a wish, but Ivan refused to give him the ball. He said, "We should be happy with what we have!" But Gonzalo would not listen. He snatched the ball and ran away to the village, and told everyone about the ball.

The villagers became greedy and started making wishes. Some wanted gold, others wanted big houses. Everyone's wishes came true. The entire village was now full of big houses and there was no place left for children to play. People became rich. They also became jealous and started fighting with each other.

Gonzalo went to Ivan and said, “Here, take your ball. I am sorry for all the trouble that I have caused.”

A few days later, Ivan’s grandpa paid him a visit. Ivan and his friends rushed to greet him. They told him all about the wishing ball and how everyone in the village had changed because of their greed. Grandpa looked at the quarrelling people and said, “Ivan, don’t you think this is the right time to make a wish?”

Ivan replied excitedly, “Of course it is, grandpa!” He looked at the ball and made his wish, “O powerful ball! We do not want big houses or wealth. Give us our huts and fields back. Let everyone be happy with what they have. We shall not be greedy ever again.”

Poof! The ball glowed and disappeared. Everything went back to as it was before and the village became a happy place once again.

Moral: Greed destroys happiness.

The Backyard Fence

Not very long ago, in a town there lived a young boy. He got angry over small matters. He fought with everyone – his friends, neighbours and even his younger sister! His parents often tried to correct his behaviour but failed.

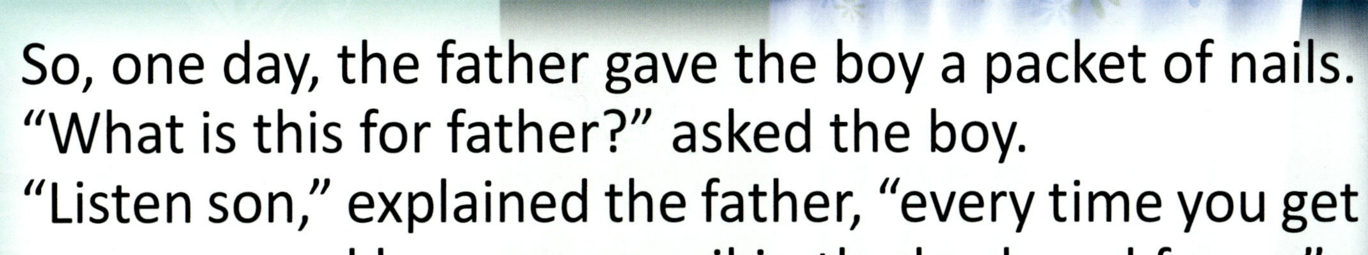

So, one day, the father gave the boy a packet of nails. "What is this for father?" asked the boy.
"Listen son," explained the father, "every time you get angry, go and hammer a nail in the backyard fence."

The next day, the boy had to drive in thirty-seven nails in the fence because he was angry that many times. “I must control my anger,” he said to himself. He made a promise to himself to control his anger at all times.

Every morning, he reminded himself of the promise he had made. As days and weeks went by, the number of nails hammered in the fence gradually went down. “It is easier to check my anger but difficult to hammer nails,” he realised.

One day, the boy did not hammer a single nail in the fence as he was able to control his anger throughout the day. The delighted boy ran up to his father and said, “Father, I did not hammer even a single nail in the fence today as I did not get angry all day.” The father was happy for his son’s changed behaviour.

"Son," said the father, "the day you do not lose your temper pull out one nail from the fence." Days passed and each day the boy pulled out a nail. Finally, all the nails on the fence were removed. The boy happily went to his father and said, "Father! I no longer feel angry. I have removed all the nails from the fence."

The father went to the fence and patted his son.

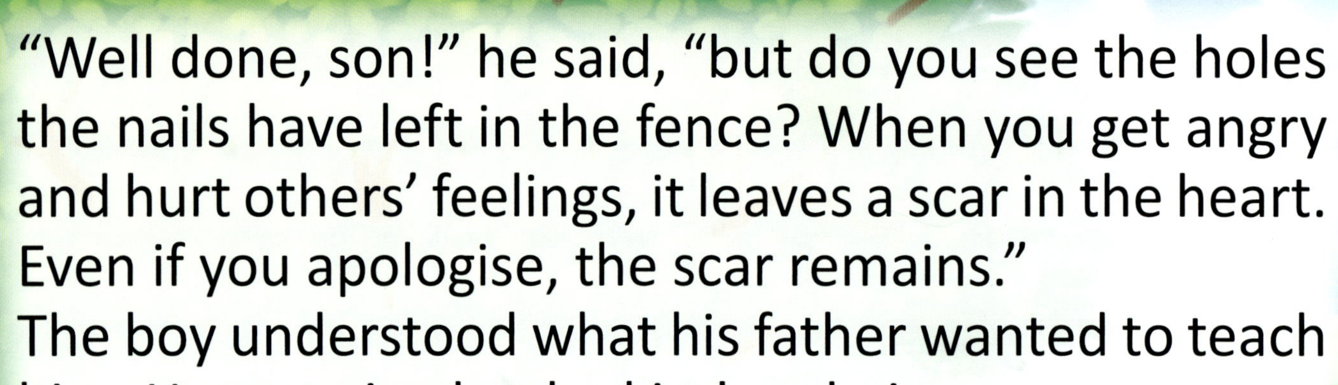

"Well done, son!" he said, "but do you see the holes the nails have left in the fence? When you get angry and hurt others' feelings, it leaves a scar in the heart. Even if you apologise, the scar remains."

The boy understood what his father wanted to teach him. He promised to be kind and nice to everyone.

Moral: **Wounds caused by angry words seldom heal.**